Disclaimer

This is a work of fiction. Any names, businesses, characters, events, incidents and places are either the product of the author's imagination or used in a fictitious manner. Any resemblance to actual people, living or dead, or actual events or occurrences is purely coincidental.

Billionaire Romance
The Billionaire's Private Island

Billionaire Island Romance Series
Book 1

By Alessandra Bancroft
Copyright © 2015

Table of Contents

Chapter 1: The Billionaire's Brilliant Idea

"Petra?" Luke called, the commanding tone in his voice irritating his long-time assistant. "I expected those dossiers delivered to me an hour ago!"

"Right," Petra yelled with exasperation in her voice. "And I expected to have all the information I needed 4 hours ago!"

Petra sighed and rolled her eyes, her fingers massaging her temples as she shut her eyes and tried to focus. Working for Luke "The Bullet" Garmount was certainly lucrative, but at moments like this she really wondered whether or not she'd be better off doing something a bit more pleasant, like living in a yurt in Outer Mongolia milking yaks. Then she'd remember that the pay was stellar, he could be quite charming and pleasant most the time, and she actually kinda liked him. Once you got past his minor God complex and imperious nature, he was actually a pretty OK dude.

Right now, Petrea wished she had a faster internet connection. The irony was not lost on her. Luke had made his billions in cloud-based services and rapid application development, but none of that mattered on this remote Caribbean island they had just relocated to. Technicians were still working to install the brand new fiber network, and they were currently having to make do with cellular data service until that work was complete. She was glad she wasn't going to be getting the data overage charges on *her* bill. Stellar pay or not, she wasn't stupid with her money. She checked the screen – only two more files to go.

"Why don't you take a swim?" she suggested. She slipped her USB drive into an open port on her laptop. "Cool your jets while I coax this dinosaur tech to do something magical?"

She was startled by the sound of his hand slapping the doorframe. "Just how much longer is this going to take?"

Petra swiveled her chair to face him. He had the looks of a high-end model – chiseled features, muscular arms, broad shoulders tapering to a narrow waist – and leaning against the doorframe with that impatient scowl on his face gave him quite an imposing look. Since they'd arrived, he'd taken to wearing little more than tight swim trunks and flip flops, and the tan lines from the casual work shirts he'd favored in California had disappeared. He had perfectly bronzed skin, wavy sandy hair, and piercing blue eyes – many women looking at him would cross their legs in delicious anticipation if he were smiling instead of scowling.

Any woman but Petra, that is, who preferred her hard bodies in her own gender. *"Too bad the boss man doesn't have a sister."* She thought. *"On the other hand, I don't even want to* think *about coping with* two *of them."*

She turned the laptop to face him and pointed to the excruciatingly slow creep of the bar indicating the slow download progress. "It's going to be a bit longer," she said, "assuming, of course, that the connection holds." She slapped the laptop back around and continued copying files to the tiny portable drive. "Swim, soak, drown. I don't care which one you choose, as long as you leave me in peace to do my work." She dismissed him with a wave of the hand.

Luke begrudgingly complied. He was strong, powerful, wealthy beyond anyone's wildest dreams, and his business sense was as keen as his sexual prowess, at least according to all the stories he loved to share with her. When he would enter a boardroom, even the hardcore corporate bullies would quake in their boots. They knew what happened when they messed with the best, as he had a terrible appetite for vengeance when crossed and would go out of his way to make examples of those who wronged him.

He was also his own man, and no one scolded him, ever – except for Petra. Only Petra could treat him like an errant ten-year-old. She'd been with him from the start of his amazing financial run, and her loyalty and work ethic had earned her the right to take the occasional liberty. She was right more often than not, and he'd learned early on that her badass business savvy came with a whole boatload of sass. She had a hell of a rack as well, which he loved to stare it, but which he knew was strictly off limits.

Heading to the pool, Luke cleared his head with a few laps around the swimming pool and then started sipping on one of Marco's delicious tropical island drinks poolside. He wasn't sure if it was the gorgeous weather or the delicious anticipation of all his plans coming together, but whatever it was made the drink taste even better than usual. He lay back in the lounge chair, sinking into the soft pillows, and fantasized about what delights the next few weeks would bring.

Ten women. Ten beautiful women. Ten gorgeous, intelligent, accomplished women, and they were all going to be all his. Well, for a time at least. He was a normal guy; the harem fantasy was definitely going through his head, presenting all sorts of interestingly debauched possibilities. It was sort of a shame he had to keep them secret from each other. It would definitely be nice to get a few of them in bed at the same time. Eventually, he supposed, he'd have to select one of them. He grinned impishly into his fruity drink; he certainly intended to make the most of the situation he'd been able to engineer while he could. He had worked like a maniac the last ten years and now it was his time for his rich reward.

He'd been lamenting his experiences in the social scene with Petra over a few too many drinks when the idea had come to him. If he was going to be surrounded by gold diggers now that the world knew his net worth, why not just pony up the cash and see if he could finally find the perfect woman for him. Petra had given him some major side-eye as he shared his plans, but she'd carried them out to the letter – despite her rather obvious doubts about his sanity – quickly finding and purchasing the perfect island property to transform into his personal playground. He'd spent millions, sparing no expense in the construction and outfitting of eleven beautiful mansions on the site, one for him and one for each of his soon to be girlfriends. The only thing he worried about was that some of the girls would find out what he was up to, as they each currently thought that they were the only one on the island with him.

The sun was warm on his skin as he closed his eyes to imagine them, these ten gorgeous women he was eager to meet. They would be stunningly beautiful, classy, and brilliant in their own fields, that much he was sure of. Petra had hired the ten most famous matchmakers in the world, promising each a small fortune if they produced the perfect match. No marriage. Luke had been clear on that score. Just playmates, women who were willing and able to match his mind and libido, and who wanted nothing more than to be his social partner for as long as the arrangement was mutually beneficial.

His fingers brushed the large gold medallion suspended around his neck from a thick golden rope chain and he played with the warm metal, feeling the outline of the bullet embossed on its surface. Carla had given it to him, her last gift to him before her death in a skiing accident, just a month before they would have been married. The loss had shredded him, a shock to his then-settled system. Petra had been his rock, making all of the funeral arrangements and quickly removing all traces of Carla from their shared home at his request after he had grieved for several months. Only this gold medallion remained, a constant reminder of the woman he'd loved and the pain he'd suffered when he'd lost his life partner. He had loved her completely. There would never be another.

He felt Petra's arrival before she spoke, her shadow palpable on his bare skin. Changed into a white bikini now, she stood before him, offering the small hard drive that contained the dossiers of the women he'd contracted to meet. "Perfect timing, as usual," he murmured as he took the drive. "My apologies for my outburst earlier. The delays on the fiber installation have been a real pain."

She nodded in agreement and acceptance, then dove into the pool. He watched her for several long moments, appreciative of her athleticism as she sped through her first lap. When it was clear she was going to get in a good workout, he wrapped a towel around his waist and headed inside to check out the files on the women he was about to meet. Before he headed in, he took one last admiring look at Petra as she swam gracefully. *"Definitely too bad that's off limits."* He thought.

After a brisk shower, Luke dressed in loose-fitting linen pants and sat on his bed. He fired up the computer, propping the remote keyboard and track pad on his lap. He got comfortable against the soft grey sand-washed silk bedding and the inlaid headboard of his antique Art Deco teak and mahogany bed and pulled up the folder of dossiers on the enormous screen across the room. Ten smiling, gorgeous faces shone out at him: Mignonne, a French attorney with an interest in skydiving; Portia, an animal activist living in Montana; Svetlana, an icy investment capitalist from Russia. There were two women named Pamela, one a farmer from Nebraska, the other a British professor of archeology. There was a Canadian named Carmen, with red hair, piercing green eyes and an impressive investment portfolio, followed by Dova, a South African school headmaster with skin dark as night. Constantine was a world class tennis player from Belgium, and Kiko was a highly-respected Japanese research chemist who indulged in the occasional bit of weekend skateboarding. Rounding out the ten was Yuna, South Korean by birth who had immigrated to the US at ten. She was...what? Were his eyes deceiving him? She was a massage therapist?

"She must be damned good," he muttered, puzzled by this last inclusion among the list of so many accomplished women, although he could not deny her beauty in the pictures. He clicked off the screen and headed down to the kitchen in search of lunch and Petra.

They spoke as they ate, Petra finalizing the details of the women's arrival plans while Luke inhaled one of Marta's special club sandwiches and grunted his approval. He'd inspected the women's quarters himself the week before. Each house — mansion, really — was outfitted with all the necessary luxuries, as well as most of the *unnecessary* luxuries. Each mansion's staff had been offered bonuses in exchange for their silence about the arrangements, with truly astronomical amounts of bonus money to follow if 'their' girl was picked, so the staff had more than ample reason to cater to their every whim. Bicycles and sporting equipment were provided at each home, and each had access to a secluded beach. They certainly wouldn't get bored and complain of nothing to do, anyway. Each was a short car ride from his home, but still several miles away from each of the others, the ten mansions fanning out in a circle from his own estate, which was located in the center of the island.

"Have you reconsidered the need for the secrecy?" Petra asked, her slender fingers delicately holding a truly decadent BLT. "It seems unfair, if you ask me, and likely to blow up in your face. Spectacularly. We're talking big budget special effects kabooms. These are smart women you know."

Luke shot her an exasperated look. "I haven't, and I don't care," he replied. "I want to get to know them as they are," he grumbled, taking a swig of his beer, "not as they think they need to be to beat out someone else." He set the bottle on the table and wiped at his mouth with a napkin. "It's like what we learned while running the tech incubator team. I need to know how they will act naturally, not with any preconceived notions or thoughts of competing against others to win him as a prize."

Petra rolled her eyes as she took a sip from her wine spritzer. "Whatever," she muttered. "Just don't come crying to me when someone spills the beans and you're surrounded by an angry mob of women waving around torches and pitchforks and screaming for your head on a platter."

"Trust me," Luke said, smiling at her confidently as he stood up from the table. "I always know exactly what I'm doing."

Chapter 2: Breathless Arrivals

From the helicopter, the island loomed large, a lush green jewel in a beautiful sea of perfect blue. Yuna pressed her nose against the glass, stomach churning from the combination of the craft's jerky movements in the slightly erratic wind and her growing nerves. This was clearly an insane idea. What on earth had she been thinking when she agreed to this? When Roki San had offered her this "once in a lifetime chance," she'd been just desperate and lonely enough to say yes. It might have been a combination of that and being enraged at another wealthy client who thought that an Asian massage therapist naturally meant that he was getting a 'happy ending' out of the transaction. She had always dreamed of a real-life fairy tale happy ending, not endless sleazy propositions from rapidly aging musicians. Now, here she was, literally approaching the doorstep of her dream, and she wanted nothing more than to turn around and go back to her nice, safe, normal, *boring* life in Modesto, California.

She clutched at the belt strapped across her body as the chopper began its descent. Roki patted her hand, gently murmuring soothing words to the young woman. She promised her safe landings, a successful conquest, and a happy future. Yuna nodded, noticing a shift in the pilot's eyes looking at her through the rear mirror in the cockpit. What had she seen in them? Amusement? Cynicism? Sympathy? Something that was all three at once? She closed her eyes and took a deep breath, gathering her courage as they seemed to almost drop from the air toward the landing pad. She was in this now.

Yuna gave Roki's hand a squeeze. "No turning back," she whispered, and the older woman gave her a sage nod in agreement.

Pamela Cartwright stared with wide eyes as she stood in the foyer of the enormous mansion. "Amazing!" she exclaimed, fists clenched at her side, her body working to contain the awe in her voice. This was such a change from the two-story Nebraska farmhouse that had been her home since birth. The marble floors and curving staircases gleamed, tall vases filled with vibrant tropical flowers filled the air with heady perfume, and the high ceilings featured large ornately rimmed skylights which made the entire place glow with warm, elegant energy. *It looks like something straight out of one of those fancy soap operas Mama loved so much.*

"This way, ma'am," said Ronald, head of the household staff. He carried her two suitcases toward the sweeping staircase.

Pam's ingrained manners stopped her, and she motioned toward the door. "Um, shouldn't we wait for Annie?"

Ronald shook his head. "She'll be joining you in half an hour. First, she has a meeting at the big house." He started up the stairs. "Please follow me."

Pam nodded, then slowly walked toward the staircase. She was still a bit wobbly on the three-inch heels Annie had insisted she start wearing, and she gripped the rail tightly as she willed her ankles to behave. She was pretty sure that her horse McGee had been more graceful when he was a newborn foal. She wished that she was wearing her soft, comfortable boots. When she reached the top of the staircase, she paused on the landing to take it all in. "It's bigger than my barn," she whispered, turning beet red when she heard Ronald's soft chuckle behind her.

"Yes, ma'am. Mr. Garmount doesn't believe in doing anything small."

She smiled nervously and nodded, tucking her hands behind her back to spin her mother's ring for comfort. "I can tell. It's like my daddy always tells me – go big or don't go at all."

Ronald smiled gently and motioned down the hall. "This way."

She soaked in the atmosphere as she followed him. Rich carpets provided a soft landing for her aching feet, and on every bit of wall her eyes saw something beautiful and new. Rich oil paintings appeared near intricately carved wood shelves holding exquisite trinkets and small sculptures. She struggled to keep her heels from sinking into the carpet, even if they weren't likely to take divots out of it like they had the lawn back home when she'd first tried walking in them. She was relieved when Ronald finally stopped in front of a slightly rustic-looking carved whitewashed door.

"Here we are, ma'am." He placed one of the bags on the floor and opened the door for her to enter. Pam let out a small gasp as she saw the room. It was perfect for her and totally out of touch with the rest of the house. Cherry stained knotty pine wainscoting was paired with honeyed tones on the walls. The massive four poster bed was made with whole deep stained logs with the branches left in place at the top to hold up a cream silk canopy, and the coverlet was cranberry and cream dupioni silk in a pattern that looked like an old-fashioned quilt. The overall effect gave her the feeling of being in an elegant version of a vacation cabin.

"The bath is through here, and the closet is here." Said Ronald as he gave her a quick tour of the room, showing her how to operate the fireplace and call down to the kitchen for anything she needed that wasn't available in the small bar in one corner of the enormous room.

Before he left, he drew her attention to a folder on the desk. "Your schedule for your visit," he said. "Mr. Garmount is looking forward to making your acquaintance."

Pam extended her hand and shook Ronald's vigorously. "Thank you so much," she said. "Please tell him that I'm looking forward to meeting him, too."

After he'd left, she quickly slipped out of the heels and wiggled her toes on the plush deep green carpet. After hours in those damned heels instead of her comfortable boots, it felt better than cool, damp grass under her bare feet. Unsure of what to do next, she unpacked, reacquainting herself with the cocktail dresses, resort wear, and lingerie which Annie had helped her purchase the week before. When she got to the pair of cutoffs and the t-shirt she'd snuck into the bottom of the suitcase, she took a deep smell. Home. She sighed and placed them at the top of the closet shelf. As long as they were there, she'd remember where she came from. She told herself that she wouldn't let herself get lost in this weird world of glamour, glitz, and sparkle.

The schedule! A brief wave of nervous tension and nausea washed over her. She hoped she hadn't already missed something. She held a hand to her stomach and bit her lower lip. Annie would be very unhappy. The matchmaker had been a close friend of her mother's, and she'd been trying to convince Pam to meet her clients for the last couple of years.

The whole idea of having a matchmaker set her up with someone made Pam self-conscious. She knew she was desirable, but she'd always been shy, preferring the company of the horses on the farm, especially her dear McGee, to any of the people she'd met. She took a long look in the mirror hanging over the desk, smoothing her dark curly hair as best she could as she opened the folder.

Tomorrow. She was free, on her own, until tomorrow, when, from the looks of things, she'd be spending the morning with Luke Garmount. She pulled out his photograph and bio. Handsome. She looked at her own image again, smooth tanned skin, bright blue eyes, hourglass figure. She wondered what she'd gotten herself into and what would be expected of her. Annie had told her she wouldn't have to do anything with him at all if she didn't want to. Her exact words had been, "He's not looking for a whore," but Pam couldn't see how she could expect to do anything but everything this wealthy man wanted if she was going to make the match Annie so desperately wanted her to make. Pam wasn't a virgin—she'd lost that years before with a sweet farmhand in the hayloft—but she wasn't *loose*, either. She looked at Garmount's picture again. *"He is kind of hot."* She thought.

"I'll think about it tomorrow," she told the figure in the mirror, then giggled and put on her best Scarlet O'Hara impression. "Tomorrow is another day."

The clicking of Svetlana's heels rang through the foyer like gunfire. "Marco," she purred, her accent thick and smoky, "show me my room. I'd like to get comfortable."

Marco silently complied, his shoulders slightly slumping under the sight of all of her bags and her icy gaze. She sniffed as she followed him up the stairs, her eyes calculating the cost of the opulence on display in the mansion. Marble, gilt, crystal. "Dull," she muttered disdainfully. Sculptures. "Unoriginal." Hand-carved bannisters. "Ordinary." Once they'd reached the carpet, the sound of her step gave way to the swish of her hips beneath the pristine white column dress she'd worn for travel. Marco said a silent prayer that the haughty woman would at least like her bedroom.

Severe was too soft a word to describe the decor, and Svetlana Petrovich felt immediately comfortable. Stark white punctuated with ebony and blood red, this was a room in which she could relax and let her hair down. *This*, finally, was a room with a modicum of taste and elegance. It *might* make up for the utterly plebian fiasco of the rest of the place. How anyone could amass a fortune of Garmount's caliber and still have execrable taste, she didn't know. She stood stock still as Marco placed her bags near the closet and nervously informed her about the room's amenities.

When he'd left, she looked at the schedule, satisfied that she had a full day to prepare for her initial dinner meeting with Luke. She checked the tiny transmitter in her white gold and diamond wristwatch, then rubbed the corner of the cheap babushka scarf her grandmother had once worn as a reminder of the price of failure. She would *not* fail, not *ever*.

Knowing that her matchmaker Helga would be arriving soon to fill her in on the details of her meeting with Garmount, she decided to freshen up. Helga demanded absolute perfection, though that was no more than the sublime impeccability Svetlana demanded of herself on any job. Svetlana could see a wisp of platinum blonde hair sneaking out of her jeweled hair clip, as she looked in the mirror. She also noticed a small chip in her deep red nail polish. She knew, too, that her legs bore the smudge marks of the black leather boots she wore. Helga's clipped voice rang out in her head. *That will not do!* She headed to the bath.

"Mignonne, I thought I told you to leave those behind!" Yelled Mignonne's matchmaker Aimee.

Aimee stared at Mignonne intently and with rising irritation as she was taking a tour of her new private mansion without even looking around. Mignonne, deeply engrossed by an open manila folder that she held in her hands, walked absently past beautiful artworks and impeccably decorated rooms, letting Aimee's words fly right over her head.

Only after Aimee angrily slapped the folder out of Mignonne's hand did she flinch and look up. Papers went flying everywhere.

"My hearing briefs!" Mignonne cried, "My client will never win this case if I don't find that precedent." She scrambled to retrieve papers as they scattered across the Aubusson runner and under an antique Queen Anne occasional table.

"You're not here to win a case, my dear," Aimee said gently, bending down to help her gather the papers. "You're here to impress a billionaire."

Mignonne was a recent graduate of Sorbonne Law School, the top law institution in Paris. Stealing a glance at herself in a fancy mirror that hung in the hallway, she critically analyzed herself. Soon her long, silky black hair would be due for a trim, her heart-shaped face due for a spa treatment and her eyebrows a wax. She took a second glance, leaning close to the mirror and peering at a single stray eyebrow hair. Overdue. She hoped that Aimee had brought tweezers along with all her other torture devices. Comparing her height to the mirror itself, she considered asking Aimee to provide her with a pair of higher-heeled shoes. The billionaire might not be interested in – or impressed by – someone so short. She sighed. She couldn't help but think ahead. It was what she was trained to do as a lawyer. Sometimes, she wished she could just focus on the present, as Aimee was trying to help her do now.

"You really work much too hard, Mignonne," Aimee said as she continued to lead her down the hallway. "It's time for you to sit back, relax and have some fun. If you worry too much about your work, you're going to age that beautiful skin of yours too quickly. You should learn to be like your sisters. They're not so serious about their work."

"I should think it quite difficult to be all that serious about being either a swimsuit model or a B-list celebrity's stylist", Mignonne thought somewhat sourly.

As they turned the corner, Mignonne stopped in her tracks. Aimee had brought her into a room that was almost completely covered with floor to ceiling hand-carved built in bookshelves. Hurrying over to one of the closest shelves, she grabbed a book and read the title. It was a law book. She was in a law library, one of the most boring places on earth to almost everyone else, but to her it was like heaven.

"Incroyable! This is incredible!" she said. She walked around the shelves, delicately caressing the spines of the books with her hand. Moving toward the end of one shelf, she came to a curtained window with thick draperies to protect the books from overexposure to sunlight. Pulling it back, she peered out the window and gazed out at the island. Far in the distance in several directions she saw some breaks in the trees, but no evidence of the development she had been told about.

"I wonder what's out there."

"You know the rules, Mignonne," Aimee reminded her. "You're not to go beyond the premises of this estate, unless you're with Mr. Garmount."

"It just doesn't make sense," Mignonne said, straining to see as far as she could while skeptical lawyer gears turned in her head. "600 acres of land, a billionaire, and I'm supposed to stay confined to a few thousand hundred square feet? I doubt it's dangerous, I can't even hear construction."

Aimee gently tugged on Mignonne's arm. "Come away from the window now, *ma cher,*" she said, holding up the schedule. "Let's go over the schedule that Mr.

Garmount has set up for you. You'll meet him late tomorrow afternoon. I believe the two of you are scheduled to go skydiving together."

Chapter 3: Let The Games Begin

"How's it going?"

Petra turned away from the wall of monitors at the sound of Luke's voice. She lowered the volume, silencing the varied voices from the houses as the women arrived and settled into their temporary homes. "They're all getting comfortable, though considering the sheer amount of primping going on, comfortable might be the wrong word for it," she said. Motioning to one of the monitors, she added, "Only problem I'm spotting is the tennis player – she seems disappointed with the quality of the courts."

Luke furrowed his brow. "Constantine? I thought you'd gotten what they requested?"

Petra nodded wearily. "I did, but now, apparently, she's training on grass." Seeing the confused expression on Luke's face, she added, "Wimbledon. She's training for Wimbledon. Big tennis tournament? They have it in London every year? It's a pretty big deal."

Luke shook his head. "Whatever. Just make it right."

Petra sighed and rolled her eyes. "Yes your lordship," she said sarcastically.

Luke sank into the chair next to her. She could see the exhaustion on his face.

"Is everything going to plan?" he asked. They still have no idea about the others... right?"

Petra shook her head affirmatively. "Everything is going perfectly. You are a true genius!"

Luke loved it when she played along with him... even though he knew it wasn't sincere.

"You know expecting that to last for long is pretty stupid, right? 600 acres is a lot of land, but voices carry." said Petra, ruining the moment.

He glared at her. "And risk their contracts? No, I think the handlers know exactly what's at stake for them if they don't follow the rules, and there is plenty of distance between them."

The rules were simple. The women had to be on birth control with up to date medical records indicating no STDs. They were forbidden to divulge the location of the island or the identity of its owner. There was to be no exploring beyond the boundaries of the estate on which they were settled. There was plenty to do and see in each area, and the cover story was that Luke was developing other parts of the island for lease as a future resort and the 'construction areas' might be dangerous. This was true, in two senses; the development was complete, the houses all occupied, but ten money-hungry women finding out that they had competition for his wallet could be pretty dangerous. A ten million dollar payout was on the line for the matchmaker – he didn't know what the matchmakers were promising his prospective companions, but he was betting it was more than worth them following the rules. Breaking the rules meant a loss of the fee altogether. Given those stakes, each handler had eagerly signed their contract, promising the handsome billionaire that he would be more than satisfied with their client.

Luke turned his attention to the screens. "So, which one do I get to meet first?"

Petra pointed to the screen at her upper left and increased the volume. The room was filled with the sounds of wheels rushing against concrete. "Kiko Yamoto, the skateboarding chemist. You're having dinner with her this evening, followed by a moonlit walk on the beach."

Luke surveyed the lithe figure on the skateboard, elbows and knees protected with pads, dark hair obscured by a safety helmet. She was flying in the custom designed skatepark. "I think she might prefer something a bit more exhilarating than a moonlit walk."

"Perhaps," Petra said, "but you're scheduled to take her snorkeling in a couple of days, so I suggest you take it slow. Remember, you've got nine other women to court this week."

Luke shook his head vigorously. "Not courting—more like interviewing."

Petra waved her hand dismissively. "You contacted matchmakers. They make matches—marriage matches. You've invited them here, surrounded them in luxury, and you're going to be dating them. You yourself know that you're planning to select one of them—"

"To be my companion."

"To be your companion," Petra continued, "to be on your arm at public events and in your bed in private. You, my dear," she jabbed a finger at his bicep, "are the billionaire bachelor." She punched a button on the control panel, and the opening credits for the popular television dating show appeared across all of the screens in the room. The romantic music swelled, and Luke didn't have to feign annoyance when the image of himself Petra had superimposed on the video appeared.

"The difference," he began, slowly and carefully choosing his words, "is that they don't know they're competing against other women. I'm just interviewing candidates—for a job."

Petra laughed heartily as she pulled up the video footage from each mansion, filling the room with the faces of the beautiful women who were at this moment preparing for their first dates with Luke. "Love is not a job, Luke. These women might be willing to go along with your rules and your contract, but I know you. Mark my words, this is not going down the way you think it will."

Luke scowled at his assistant, anger barely contained beneath the surface of his skin. "Do what I pay you to do, and keep your opinions to yourself." He said heatedly. He stood up and glared at her... his eyes a steely blue. "I am trying to be remembered for a thousand years and if I am going to do that I need things to go the way I planned them!" He boomed in a powerful voice, then stormed out of the room and in the direction of the gym. Petra felt a bit weak in the knees. It had been sometime since he had yelled at her like that, and it was quite intimidating. Guess it was time to play nice for a bit.

Luke angrily walked into the gym. He needed to focus on something other than Petra's words, and nothing commanded his focus like lifting heavy weight. As he added two hundred fifty pounds to the bar, despite his trainer's skeptically raised eyebrow, he felt more and more control returning. He didn't want love, wasn't looking for love. Love had come with Carla and her death had torn his heart right out of his chest. Love was not for him then and it wasn't for him now. His life was so altered from those days that he could never trust that the women he met wanted *him* and not his money. This was the right course. He would find a suitable companion, one who could be the woman in his life with no expectations of commitments of the heart. Someone he could control and who would be totally loyal. He told himself that he wouldn't care if she saw him as a walking wallet. It wouldn't matter, so long as she was helping him become one of the greatest men who had ever lived!

He exhaled sharply each time he pushed the weights from his chest, under the watchful eye of his trainer. After thirty minutes of heavy lifting the clock on the wall told him it was time to get ready for his first date, and he smiled. Adrenaline coursing through his veins and feeling much better, he high-fived his trainer as he left the gym. "Let the games begin!"

Chapter 4: Yuna in Paradise

She didn't feel out of place in the mansion, not exactly. Yuna had been in too many houses of this size to feel overwhelmed or uncomfortable. She was no stranger to wealth ostentatiously on display. Her clients were wealthy to varying degrees, and she'd spent just as much time in the outrageously decorated and pretentious mansions of music stars as she had in the more tastefully appointed homes of various rich professionals.

She could hear her mother's voice in her head, telling her young self that she deserved "everything good the world has to offer." She wondered at times what her mother would think of her now, what she would say about her profession and life if she was still alive. In these moments, Yuna often decided that her mother would be happy about her education and proud of her academic accomplishments — a Master's in biology from Stanford that she had completed two years early, but she thought her mother would be concerned and disappointed by exactly how Yuna was putting that education to work, and probably irritated that her only daughter had no romantic prospects to speak of and no children.

Yuna could almost hear her mother's most likely reaction. *Why didn't you go to medical school? You could of been a doctor by now, meeting handsome eligible doctors every day. You might of even be married!*

"Best in the massage business and still not good enough," Yuna grumbled. At least she could tell her mother's memory that she was doing something about meeting someone handsome and eligible. She wandered through the rooms, taking in every bit of this place that she'd call home for a few weeks. The energy in some spaces felt all wrong. However, taken as a whole, she approved of the decor and furnishings. The rest she'd alter to neutralize the tensions she felt in various corners.

The dining and living areas were contemporary and tasteful. Spare, clean lines were softened by gentle curving edges throughout the space. She paused in the kitchen for a snack, thrilled to find traditional Korean snacks and foods alongside some of her American favorites. She decided against sampling the honey candy, but took a few pieces of fresh sushi and some pineapple juice as she continued on her tour of the home.

The therapy room nearly brought her to tears. She'd always dreamed of something like this, but to see it realized—and available to her in this space where she was sure she'd have little use of it—was almost too much. Low lighting highlighted the rich warm tones of the meticulously cut, deceptively simple, glorious hand-oiled teak furnishings. On one side was a deep, luxurious, Carrera marble tub for spa treatments, its beautiful gloss offset perfectly by simply elegant hammered copper fixtures. The table, indisputably the centerpiece of the room, was comfortable and of the best quality. Above it hung two parallel bars, and she smiled. She loved walking on clients' backs when asked to, and her clients seemed to request this a great deal.

Her matchmaker, Roki San, found her unpacking her oils and scrubs into one of the beautifully oiled teak cabinets near the table. "You like?"

Yuna looked up, giggled, and nodded. At just over sixty, short, and plump, Roki San presented the expected face of an Asian matchmaker, and she used that expectation to broker enormous profits for herself. Yuna had watched her work as a child, spending afternoons with the older woman after school to improve her English while Roki switched between the broken English with which she addressed white clients to the flawless Korean speech she reserved for those she knew best. "It makes them comfortable to see and hear what they expect," she had told Yuna one day, "and comfortable people are so much more agreeable than suspicious ones–and far more likely to spend money." When Yuna questioned her about the ethics of her work, Roki had shrugged. "I see into their hearts and souls. I know what they want—the women and the men—and I give them what they want, sometimes before they realize it themselves. There is a science to it, and there is an art to making a match. But to make money from it? That, dear child, requires a bit more finesse. It's more of a natural talent if you ask me. You are either born with it or your not."

Finesse was definitely a word Yuna would use to describe Roki at the moment. She watched as the woman ran a hot bath in the spa tub, then disrobed and settled in. When she was comfortably situated, she motioned for Yuna to join her. Yuna removed her sandals and perched on the edge of the tub, dangling her toes in the fragrant water, watching steam rise and wreath her ankles. Roki took Yuna's hand and looked thoughtfully at her before sighing.

"He seems unsuitable for you, my dear, but appearances at first can deceive, can they not? There is something hidden there; perhaps it will do simply to figure out what is beneath before we cast this one aside." Her warm eyes found Yuna's sad ones, and she reached up to give her a motherly stroke on the cheek. "When I first met him he seemed...," she paused, choosing her words carefully, "broken, like a bird that has had its feathers clipped."

Chapter 5: Kiko in the Moonlight

As Luke got ready for an evening with his first candidate, Kiko, he gazed into the long mirror in his lavish bathroom and admired himself. The six-pack abs he paid his trainer to bring out in him at least meant that he wouldn't be sucking in his gut all night long. He knew he was good-looking, but starting to *really* date again had him looking at himself critically. He was completely naked, except for the towel wrapped around his waist and the large gold bullet medallion around his neck. Petra's words from earlier rang out in his mind. *"Mark my words, this is not going down the way you think it will."* Feeling the weight of the medallion and the bittersweet memories attached to it against his chest, he quickly squashed those words aside and continued to get ready, changing into one of his finest tailored suits. It was show time.

Meanwhile, Kiko's matchmaker Kaito was helping her prepare for the evening as well. Instead of Kiko's preferred traditional Japanese kimono and obi, Kaito had picked out some rather revealing clothes that were closer to the current American trends, with an eye to the large reward she would receive if Luke selected her girl. Though Kiko was reluctant to wear clothes of such a suggestive nature, she put them on anyway.

"I don't know about this," Kiko said as she pulled the tight pair of shorts around her skinny waist. "Aren't these kind of...?"

"These clothes will help you succeed," Kaito insisted. "You've got to give it all you have. Success does not find the half-hearted." Peeking out behind the curtain, she saw the two headlights from Luke's limousine bounce off the windowpanes. "Mr. Garmount has arrived!"

Kiko flashed a smile, but felt butterflies explode in her belly. Though she was a very intelligent and successful woman, she was also very shy in nature when it came to social interactions. "You'll introduce me, right?"

"Yes," Kaito replied, brushing the bangs out of the rest of Kiko's hair and onto her wide forehead as a finishing touch, artfully framing her deep brown eyes. "Don't be nervous. You'll do great. I'll be here to coach you every step of the way."

A powerful knock rang out on the other side of the front door. Kaito left Kiko standing in the middle of the foyer nervously as she ran to answer it. Kiko's stomach did flip flops as Kaito swung the door open. Luke stood tall, confident and handsome on the front porch, holding a large bouquet of beautiful, colorful flowers.

"Hello Kiko," he smiled and looked her directly in the eyes as he stepped inside and approached her.

Kiko smiled faintly. "Hello."

"You look gorgeous!" Luke said as he handed her the flowers and gave her a small kiss on the cheek. He held out his arm. "Let's get going, shall we? I believe we're going to enjoy a wonderful dinner together. After that, we'll take a relaxing, romantic moonlit walk along my private stretch of beach."

After having a delicious, traditional Japanese style dinner together, and sharing drinks and laughs, Luke found himself walking under the moonlight with Kiko. The night was balmy with just the hint of a breeze stirring strands of long hair around her lovely face, and the moonlight made her skin glow like a precious pearl. He smelled the alluring jasmine and amber of her perfume and looked at the doll-like perfection of her figure. He felt his blood warming, thinking of her writhing beneath him. He could almost hear her moans.

They loosely held hands as they left a trail of footprints along the edge of the water. He tried to think of something debonair to say.

"How is your house?" Luke asked. "Did you find everything to your satisfaction?"

"I wouldn't exactly call it a house," Kiko giggled. "More like a mansion. It's bigger than any building that I've studied in at the University."

"How are the conditions of the skate park?"

"Amazing, thank you," Kiko smiled. "I've always dreamed of having my own private skate park. Ever since I was a little girl, I've always found skateboarding to be the most exhilarating experience."

Luke stopped short and turned to Kiko. Gazing at her in the outfit that Kaito had picked out, his eyes grew big like a little boy on Christmas morning. *And, oh, would I ever love to unwrap this present....* "Do you know what I find exhilarating, Kiko?"

"What?"

Luke reached up to her face to brush her bangs to the side. "You, in that stunning outfit of yours. You're a chemist, so tell me, what two elements are needed to make a romantic connection?"

Luke's hands felt warm against her palm and face. Having such a handsome, rich man staring into her eyes made her nervous yet excited. Normally, when a person asked her a chemistry question, she immediately turned to facts for an answer. She had invented processes that created alloys prized in the industry. She knew her business when it came to chemistry and was confident around other chemists. She could give enthralling lectures at chemistry symposiums, never fumbling for a word. Now, knowing that Luke was just being metaphorical, she felt awkward and shy. She struggled to reply with a witty answer.

After a few moments, she smiled faintly and replied with, "You and me."

"I like those two elements," said Luke as smiled back and felt himself starting to get hard.

For a few seconds, they stood there silently, gazing into each other's eyes. Then, like magnets coming together, they both began to lean in toward each other, Kiko puffing her lips out a bit for a kiss. Just as Luke dipped his head, he suddenly heard the ringing of his cell phone. It seemed to startle Kiko and she pulled back a bit to Luke's dismay. *This phone is only to be used in emergencies.* He thought.

"Excuse me," he said sheepishly as he pulled out his phone and answered with a voice full of irritation.

"Petra? Yes?" Kiko couldn't make out what Petra was saying on the other line but after a few seconds Luke grumbled and said, "Yes, I see."

Hanging up, he looked at her with a pout that was entirely too charming. "I hate to cut our evening short, Kiko, but I have been summoned back to my quarters for some unexpected business troubles."

He gently took her hand and looked her in the eyes. "Not to worry, though. The two of us are going snorkeling in a few days and I'm sure we can pick up right where we left off." He could see the disappointment in her eyes as he kissed her on her the lips. She kissed him back, but he knew it just wasn't the same as it would have been if he wasn't interrupted.

After seeing Kiko back to her mansion, Luke returned to his own home where Petra was waiting in the foyer, with dark thoughts in his head of throwing his cell phone into the sea.

"How dare you interrupt, Petra?" Luke growled. "We were just about to have the best kiss ever... and then who knows what! I told you this phone is for emergency calls only."

"I told you to take it slow, remember?" Petra crossed her arms. "You have at least two more dates with her."

"Interviews!" Luke bellowed.

Petra ignored his correction. "Besides, you know what they say about women who have sex on the first date. Don't be that guy who expects it and gets all pissy when he doesn't get it."

Luke took a deep breath, thinking about that for a moment. What *would* he think of a woman who slept with him on the first date? *Honestly? First thing through my head would probably be 'hell yeah!', but after that? Would I still want a girl who wasn't even a challenge?* "Yes, Petra, you're absolutely right," he apologized. "I do tend to jump into things a lot, don't I? It's just that I've been single for so long!"

"Glad you're finally coming to your senses," Petra said. "Now why don't you get some rest? You'll be meeting with the next girl, Pam, tomorrow. Remember — slow!"

Chapter 6: Riding with Pam

Pam rubbed her eyes and gazed into the mirror over the bathroom sink, wincing at the bags under her eyes. She tried to get a good night's sleep but all of the excitement and glamour, plus nervousness about meeting Mr. Garmount, had caused her to toss and turn all night. On top of all that, she was also homesick. She missed her prized stallion, McGee, and the smell of Daddy's leather chair and his clouds of pipe smoke on the wide front porch.

As she dampened a washcloth in the water and applied it to her face, she heard a knock at the door from her matchmaker Annie. "Pam? Are you almost ready to meet Mr. Garmount?"

"Hardly," she joked. "I look like a total zombie. I think I might've slept fifteen minutes the whole night."

The doorknob slowly turned and Annie popped her head in before opening the door completely. "I'll be able to fix you up in no time," she said confidently. A few seconds later, she had her entire inventory of brushes, make up and other glamorous tools spread out on the counter.

"Do I really have to get all dolled up like this?" Pam asked nervously. "My daddy always told me to find a man who would fall in love with my mind, not my looks."

"It's true, looks aren't everything," Annie admitted with a sigh. She then gave Pam's hair a hard brush, causing her to jerk. "But it does count for a lot. Don't kid yourself, men think with two brains, and pleasing the eyes is guaranteed to stir the brain that really makes all the decisions for them. Still, don't worry yourself. I am *sure* Mr. Garmount will go crazy over your sweet personality."

A few hours later, Pam was almost ready to go. She and Annie were practicing perfecting the art of walking in heels when the doorbell rang. "That must be him!" Annie exclaimed, running to the door. Swinging it open, there stood Luke, looking just as handsome as the night before. "Hello again, Mr. Garmount!"

When Annie moved away from the door, Pam stole a look. She couldn't believe her eyes. Luke was wearing a pair of dark blue jeans, a tightly fitted flannel shirt and a brown leather cowboy hat that made his bright blue eyes stand out below. Pam hadn't expected his choice of clothing at all and was almost tempted to run back upstairs and change into the comfortable old clothes that she had snuck in from home.

Pam hobbled and lurched her way over to him and shook his hand. "It's a pleasure to meet you, Mr. Garmount," she beamed.

"Likewise," Luke replied, squeezing her hand. It felt so big, warm and powerful to her. "It's a beautiful day for spending some time at my private ranch. Let's get going!"

A short and smooth limo ride later, as Luke had put in professional roads throughout the island, the made it to Luke's private ranch, a stretch of farm that he had set up on an open field on the island. He knew, (Thanks to all of Petras research), that she would fall in love with it instantly. Luke opened the door for her. As she got out, she marveled at the sight of it – it was just like home, just a bit smaller. There was a large red barn and several brown horses poking their heads over stall doors. From a glance, they were good stock, even if none could hold a candle to her horse McGee. Next to it, a fenced field held several cows. Pigs oinked contentedly in a fenced wallow on the other side of the barn. A few chickens wandered about the property, clucking quietly as if talking to themselves, pecking the ground every couple of feet. A rooster flapped his wings to boost himself onto a fence post and crowed his ownership of his feathery little harem.

"It's beautiful!" Pam exclaimed, beaming with excitement.

"You're beautiful," Luke said, watching her with a smile and truly admiring her. "I couldn't help but notice that from the second I saw you."

Pam smiled and giggled softly. "You're so flattering, Mr. Garmount."

"Please, call me Luke."

"Luke," she said a bit more sexily than she had intended.

Luke motioned over to barn. "What do you say we go on a nice horseback ride through the fields here on my island? The views are quite spectacular." He really wanted to say, *Why don't we head back to the hayloft and do it doggy style, I promise to be spectacular – repeatedly,* but he bit his tongue, remembering what he promised Petra after his date with Kiko.

Chapter 7: Dining with Svetlana

"So how did it go?" Petra asked as soon as he came through the door.

Exhausted and sweaty, Luke leaned against the banister of the staircase that led to the second floor and smiled. "I took your advice."

Petra clapped her hands. "Good!"

His eyes suddenly flashed mischievously. "God, she has a nice rack, though."

Petra just shook her head in amusement, knowing that Luke would never really change anytime soon.

"So who am I seeing tomorrow?" he asked eagerly.

"Svetlana," Petra replied. "The Russian investor. Be careful, Luke. She's *very* beautiful, and about as cold as the iceberg that sank the *Titanic*. If I had some of my more recent reports on her a few weeks ago I would of insisted on someone else. However, on paper, she is exactly what you have been asking for."

"I do love a Russian accent whispering into my ear," Luke confessed. "Russia does have some incredibly beautiful women! "Taking the first step on the staircase, he turned to Petra and said, "I better take a shower and get cleaned up if I'm going to be meeting such a vision of beauty tomorrow. Who knows, if I don't smell like a horse I might even be able to melt her." said Luke, looking Petra directly in her eyes as he flashed one of his most confident smiles. He loved seeing her reactions, and he was not disappointed. Chuckling, Luke headed off to bed with a smile on his face.

The next morning, Svetlana began her preparations early for her meeting with Luke. Helga's words rang out in her mind as she pulled her hair back and looked in the mirror. *Everything must be perfect!*

Helga entered the room and eyed Svetlana down, circling her like a shark in the water. "Change that shirt!" she demanded, noticing a small stray string of cotton sticking out from the side. "A billionaire will never look at you like the powerful woman you are if your clothes are frayed!"

Svetlana quickly changed her entire outfit and let Helga evaluate it again. The woman might be abrupt, but she did have an excellent eye for detail. Svetlana knew without a doubt that it was the details of a deal that made it a success or failure, and she had no intention of failing–*ever*.

"Where do you think he invests his money?" Svetlana asked idly while Helga circled her like a shark.

"I told you," Helga snapped. "I don't know. You'll have to find that out for yourself. That's why you must be pristine. You cannot catch *this* kind of rich man with anything less than absolute, flawless, perfection." Helga punctuated her words with a stinging slap against Svetlana's perfectly shaped ass.

Later that night, Luke found himself dining with Svetlana over the finest Russian cuisine. Petra and her pictures weren't lying–she *was* beautiful–beautiful beyond belief, yet very serious. He was handsome and was fully aware of it, but Luke liked to let loose and play around, usually through his corny pick-up lines. He learned Svetlana was harder to charm than any woman he had ever met in his life. He could usually get even Petra to smile when she was in a foul mood, but he didn't think a wizard with a magic wand could break this icy spell; corny definitely wasn't going to cut it. She did look sexy though, and she had some kind of innate magnetic allure he could not deny. "*Am I good enough to charm her?*" he thought absently, trying to think of what he could do to impress her.

"How is your food?" Luke asked as he sipped on a glass of wine, analyzing her body with excited eyes.

Svetlana used her fork to play with the remainders of her dinner on her plate. "I've had better," she replied flatly.

Luke nearly choked on his wine. "Could I get you something else?" he offered. "I only want the best for the woman I'm courting. I just don't want to see a woman as beautiful as yourself unsatisfied."

"Its fine," she said, pushing her plate away. She leaned forward. "Tell me, Mr. Garmount...."

"You can call me Luke."

"Mr. Garmount," Svetlana continued, lowering her eyelids to give him an icy stare. "What is it that you invest your money in?"

"Well," Luke said, wiping his face with a napkin. He wasn't surprised that she brought up money because that's what most women did with him, but it had taken him a little off-guard since he had been having so much fun with the other girls so far, and none of *them* had brought up his fortune *or* how he happened to come by it. "I mostly put my money into new technology or technological start-ups. Eventually a bigger tech company comes along and buys the product or business, and I get a large portion of the profits plus a large amount of recurring passive income through royalties."

"Why technology?" Svetlana asked.

"We're living in the digital age," Luke explained, feeling like he was at one of his press conferences. "Technology is ever-changing. It is the future. I've been working with computers and technology since I was a kid. I made my first web page at nine years old and was writing code for my own programs three years later. It's my passion."

"Have you ever considered investing your money into Russian stocks?"

Luke made a face. "Well…"

Svetlana cut him off. "Our stocks had a massive growth between 2001 and 2006, Mr. Garmount, and they are poised for another boom as we speak."

Luke glanced at his watch, this is not the way he had planned their date. They had only been out for an hour and a half, but it felt more like twenty to life. And they still had several dates to go. This woman was either going to bore him to death or freeze him dead before he could get through the full four hours, never mind an entire series of dates. *Where was Petra with an interrupting phone call when you needed her?* he thought as he finished the rest of his beer in one mighty swig.

"Svetlana," Luke said, pulling his chair out from the table. "Forgive me, but I just realized that I have a couple of business proposals that I need to get out by tonight." He waited in suspense for her reaction but it had taken her so off-guard that she didn't really have one. "We can talk about this more the next time we meet. I really do apologize, but it's quite urgent."

After seeing an obviously angry Svetlana back to the limo, Luke breathed a sigh of relief and called Petra to have them send over his personal Ferrari sports car to pick him up. A few minutes later his personal trainer showed up and gave him an exhilarating ride back to his stronghold. Petra was there waiting at the entrance with her hands crossed.

"*You* copped out?" she teased with a huge smirk on her face. "Luke 'The Bullet' Garmount copped out on a date?"

Luke waved her off. "It was nowhere near a date, Petra. There was no flirting, definitely *no* fun, and she didn't want to discuss anything but my investments and the stock market in Russia! I felt more like I was talking to a potential business partner than the woman of my dreams."

"You said it yourself – it's not like you're going to be marrying her."

"Yes, but at least when I'm with the others, I feel a bit more alive and playful…like there's some sort of mental connection there, maybe even a spark, even though it'll never match up to what I had with Carla. But this one – there was nothing. Not even a spark. She was beautiful, but I'm not even sure I would have done anything with her."

"Now you're just being dramatic." said Petra.

Luke shook his head. "Whatever. I'm going to bed. This night was a train wreck."

"Don't get discouraged, Luke," Petra said and gently touched his shoulder. "She was only one girl. Tomorrow is another day."

"What have I got planned for tomorrow?"

"You're going to go skydiving with Mignonne. That should cheer you up!"

Chapter 8: Skydiving with Mignonne

Luke awoke the next morning feeling better. Sometimes all it took was a good night's sleep to forget everything. He prepared himself for his date later that morning. Pushing aside his best suit, he pulled out a tightly-fitting outfit that showed off his body. He was very excited to be falling through the sky with a beautiful woman at his side.

Luke showed up to Mignonne's mansion and swept her off her feet with his killer physique, some sincere compliments on her beauty, and the crooked grin he knew for a fact was devastating to the opposite sex, almost daring them to kiss him. Her dazed smile in return was all he needed for his self-confidence to soar again. He brought her to a private stretch of beach where they boarded a helicopter and geared up for their first skydiving adventure. Though they had only known each other for a few minutes, it was already going much better than his encounter with Svetlana.

"I can't believe how huge this island is!" Mignonne yelled over the roaring noise of the helicopter as she poked her head out of one of the windows. "I've never skydived down to something so majestic."

"Not even jumping down to the Eiffel Tower?" Luke smiled, his crooked grin putting stars in her eyes. "If we were in France, I would have you jump down to the tower and be waiting for you with a romantic candlelit dinner."

"That would be quite a presentation," Mignonne smiled, her eyes full of the future. She was so mesmerized in the moment she barely even noticed all the buildings on the island below.

A few moments later, the helicopter slowed to a stop where they were supposed to jump out.

Luke gazed at Mignonne and brushed a piece of her hair out of her goggles. "Nervous?"

"No way," she replied confidently. "I love a good thrill."

"So do I. Perhaps the rest of the day will be as thrilling as this. Well, here goes nothing!"

Luke jumped out of the plane first, followed by Mignonne, who showed no hesitation. They both plunged through the warm air, enjoying the moment. Their hearts raced and there was nothing for miles around but beautiful blue ocean with the island in the middle. After a long minute they both hit their parachutes at almost the same time and gently glided down to the beautiful white sand beach below.

"Wow!" Luke breathed out as he safely landed on the soft sand and watched Mignonne glide to a perfect landing just ahead of him. He threw his hands into the air and let out a whoop. Though none of these women could ever replace his beloved Carla, his constant adventures with them had been making him feel distracted and alive for the first time in months. Hid blood was pounding and he was feeling like "The Bullet" that had shattered his enemies and made himself a fortune! "That was exhilarating!" Luke exclaimed excitedly. "I haven't had this much fun in months!" Mignonne turned towards him with a huge smile on her face as well. "That was just perfect" she exclaimed joyfully as she hopped on over to Luke and gave him a juicy kiss on the lips. Luke was ready and kissed her back eagerly.

After a few moments Mignonne asked "I thought you were developing the rest of this island for a resort?"

Luke's happy expression quickly disappeared and his eyebrows went up. He wasn't expecting an answer like that. What made her ask? Had she figured out his secret? His body went tense and rigid. "I am."

"Then why is your mansion surrounded by ten others?" Mignonne demanded, crossing her arms over her chest. "I saw them when I was coming down."

Sweat began to form on Luke's forehead and in his palms as he tried to think of a smart answer. Petra had warned him about this but he hadn't cared at the time. He had wanted to go skydiving and that was that. Now he was regretting his decision. "Don't worry about those!" he finally snapped, more harshly than he had intended. His recent sky dive had him full of adrenaline. Turning, he paced around the beach for a few minutes before looking at the exasperated–bordering on truly angry–expression on her face.

"I apologize," Luke said, reaching out for her hand. "Those are just the headquarters for each section of the resort," he lied. "I've just been under so much stress recently that the last thing I want to think about is work. All I want to focus on right now is you."

"Oh," Mignonne responded softly, not seeming very impressed.

The rest of the date was quiet and awkward for both of them. Luckily, they had already gotten through the majority of their time together. As Luke returned Mignonne to her doorstep, she barely uttered a goodbye. She didn't trust him enough to be well-mannered, and her mind was more focused on what she had seen from the sky...the nine other houses.

Chapter 9: The Secret

"The whole secret is at risk!" Luke complained to Petra as he paced back and forth in his study. He fiercely punched the wall nearest to him, causing Petra to flinch. Luke covered his face with his hand. "I tried to distract her on the way up, but I can't believe I didn't think of what she would see after jumping out of that helicopter! I thought she'd be going too fast to notice!"

"I hate to say it, but–I told you so, Luke," Petra said squarely after she recovered from his bout of rage. "I know you had good intentions, but you should've told them all the truth from the start. Then you wouldn't be in this mess."

Luke snapped his neck toward her. "No! The last thing I need is a snake infecting my paradise!"

His words were cut off by the loud, booming doorbell that he had installed himself a few months ago.

Petra stood up to the window and pulled the curtain back. At this point, she almost had to hold in a laugh. "I think you're a little late on that, boss. The snakes have already taken hold of your paradise, and they look to be in a biting mood. "

Luke momentarily calmed down. "What do you mean?"

"See for yourself." Petra pulled the curtain back all the way to reveal twenty people gathered on his lawn–his ten girls and their respective matchmakers. The girls wore outraged expressions on their faces and the matchmakers were bickering with one another.

Helga pointed at Kaito. "Did you know about this?" she viciously spat. Kaito backed away with wide eyes. Helga turned and actually poked Roki San. "How about you?" She continued to accuse each one.

"It seems suspect to *me* that you're doing so much accusing! Perhaps *you* knew all about this... this debacle!" Aimee shouted back in the Russian matchmaker's face when confronted.

"I never would have agreed to this if I knew about this!" Constantine yelled. "This big billionaire bachelor is nothing but a player! He set us all up here as some sort of sick harem fantasy!"

For once, all twenty of them nodded their head and muttered together in agreement. Yuna stood amongst the crowd, silent yet bearing a sad expression on her face. Luke was startled by a loud thudding at his front door after watching them intently.

"Open up you stinking cheat!" Svetlana yelled. "We know you're in there!"

Luke threw his hands up in defeat as Petra dropped the curtain back into place. "What do I do, Petra?"

Petra crossed her arms sarcastically. "You should have listened to me, that's what you *should* have done. But, now is now. I know you and you can be a bit pig-headed. I also know what you've been going through since Carla. So, I suggest you take my next piece of advice. You're going to have to face them, Luke. You have to go out there and address this, if you want anything positive to come out of this at all. Now."

"Face them?" He eyed the window in paranoia. "It's just me versus twenty women!"

"You're Luke 'The Bullet' Garmount!" Petra pointed at the door. "Luke 'The Bullet' would never let a large group of women stand in his way because of a misunderstanding! You've faced down wild nerd herds and angry stockholders! You single handedly crushed the mighty Barion Moonshavent and exposed him for the fraud he is. Besides, if you don't do something now you're going to lose. Then the rest of your life you will have to deal with the fact that you spent 300 million dollars and couldn't even land one of the women!" Petra knew him well, and knew that the last statement would drive him to action. Luke hated to lose!

Luke nodded silently, suddenly going into his alter ego "The Bullet." Suddenly Luke was in the zone. He squared his shoulders, his posture straightened and the look in his eyes went to hardened blue steel. Looking at him, Petra congratulated herself on her motivational abilities. This was the man who she had seen take on the world and win time and time again.

There was another few thuds at the door, but they were singular, as if the women were starting to throw things.

"You better get out there."

"You're right." Replied Luke instantly as he strode for the front door confidently.

A few moments later, the crowd hushed as they saw Luke's front door quickly open. Luke walked out, shadowed by his two massive bodyguards Maximillion and Sven. He had barely noticed them when he walked towards the door, as they were such a regular part of his life, but was regretting walking out with them now. He already knew all his guests where unarmed and that he could probably beat all 20 of them in a fist fight.

"We want answers!" Mignonne yelled.

"What is this all about? I haven't even seen the guy yet and I've been here for 3 days!" Portia asked.

Luke stood there bug-eyed and sweating profusely. He'd survived many things in his life, including a tour in the navy, numerous natural disasters and he even got lost in the woods during a wildfire once. He'd faced down dozens of programmers complaining that the requirements he wanted weren't even possible. He'd stood up to stockholders outraged that the tech budget hadn't been slashed to get them more return. Having to face an angry mob of women was probably right up there as one of the most nerve-wracking experiences he'd ever gotten himself into. He finally raised his hands to silence the crowd.

"Ladies, ladies," he began. "What we have here is a simple misunderstanding...."

"Misunderstanding?" one of the matchmakers snapped. "Ten matchmakers and ten girls? You can't hide your intentions behind pretty words and claims of innocent miscommunication, Mr. Garmount. You've been playing all of us!"

Luke bowed his head. "I'm afraid it's true. I have some explaining to do. After the sudden and untimely death of my fiancée, Carla, I've been rather lonely. Wealth is all very well and good, but it gets boring with no one to enjoy it with. I've had numerous propositions from beautiful women, much like yourselves, but I had always felt they were just gold diggers. I wanted a companion, but the social whirl didn't seem to be the right place to find her. So I bought this private island and contacted ten of the world's best matchmakers to help me find the 'right' companion, using the incentive of a ten million dollar cash prize for the matchmaker who brought me the right woman."

As the women listened to Luke's explanation, most of their jaws dropped in shock, quickly replaced with a look of sheer disgust. Each looked at each other and whispered amongst themselves, astounded at what they were hearing. Two of the girls split their glares between Luke and their respective matchmaker, not having been filled in on just how *much* their matchmaking fee was.

"I kept you all a secret from each other because I wanted to get to know each of you for who you really are, not as a person in a competition. I really wanted each of you to behave the way you would have as if you were the only girl in my life, not worrying about what another girl might be doing. But, I guess those plans are going to be changing."

"You're damned right that those plans are going to be changing!" One of the girls yelled from the audience, and soon they were all joining in.

"Don't try giving us that 'only girl in my life' routine, buddy, we all know what you really wanted!"

"Yeah! None of us are going to want you after all this! This is all just some sick playboy's little King of the Island fantasy and we're not going to put up with it!"

Several of the matchmakers tried to shut up their charges with little success.

"Luke," Annie said. "Things have gone horribly wrong. None of our girls are going to even want to look after you now that they've heard all that."

"I understand," Luke replied sadly, putting on his best puppy dog face.

"And no matchmaker is ever going to want to do business with you."

"I think all ten matchmakers should sit down and talk," Kaito pointed out heatedly. "We've all wasted our time, money and other resources to be here while we could be out actually matching clients together. Clients who, I point out, are open and honest about their intentions from the start. But perhaps there is a way to make the best out of this mess."

"Fine, fine!" Luke said desperately. "Anything you want! I'll even let you use my private conference room." Turning behind him, he pressed the intercom on the front door panel. "Petra, please see the matchmakers to my private conference room on level one."

A few moments later, Petra herded the angry, squabbling matchmakers inside, leaving Luke by himself with the other half of the mob. *How could I have been so stupid? I even asked for intelligent women! How did I not see this coming a mile away?* He berated himself as he tried to keep his cool. *"Of course, there's always a slip up in every secret situation."* Luke thought. *Petra has been my assistant for all this time. I should have just listened to her! I'm about to be out millions, as well as out of a companion. Worst of all... I am about to become a big time loser! Come on Bullet... what's the plan?"*

Luke had plenty of time to think and berate himself as he waited anxiously outside of the conference room. Thirty minutes later they summoned Luke and the other women inside to make their announcement.

"We've come to an agreement!" said Annie.

The girls on the front lawn cheered in unison.

"I hope it involves tar and feathers," one of the girls said darkly, but Luke couldn't tell which of the lovely women had spoken. He would have to check the video tapes on that later on.

Annie gave the girls a quelling look, then raised her voice to be heard by everyone. "Since Mr. Garmount has already wasted our time, we've decided that each of our girls will have an equal shot, since we're all already here on the island," she explained, glaring back at him over her shoulder.

"Instead of having multiple dates, Mr. Garmount will meet one time with everyone he hasn't yet met, over the next six days. After everyone has had some time together, five girls will be eliminated. Then it will be up to Mr. Garmount to pick from the remaining five girls. The *winner* of Mr. Garmount's little *contest*," Annie paused to give Luke a look that said he was lower than a toad's balls, "Will receive not ten but *twenty* million dollars, split between matchmaker and match and five hundred thousand dollars split between matchmaker and match for all the others."

"This is the first time anything like this has happened in matchmaking history, but we believe it will be the best way to make the most out of this situation," Kaito added.

All twenty women murmured in grudging agreement as Luke stood there, feeling about one inch tall and more than a little like a jackass. An extra ten million down the drain was just 1 month of interest on his savings accounts, besides... he would pay ten times as much to come out of this with what he wanted.

"So what will it be, Luke? Do we have a deal?" asked Annie.

Luke heard the implied threat in her voice but had already made his decision. He put on his most confident smile, the one that drove Petra crazy, and said loudly "Deal!"

The matchmakers rejoined their charges, and Yuna turned to Roki San. "He doesn't seem very earnest," she said sadly.

Roki gently nodded and smiled. "I think Mr. Garmount will learn a great deal from his mistake."

To Be Continued...

My Other Books and Audio Books

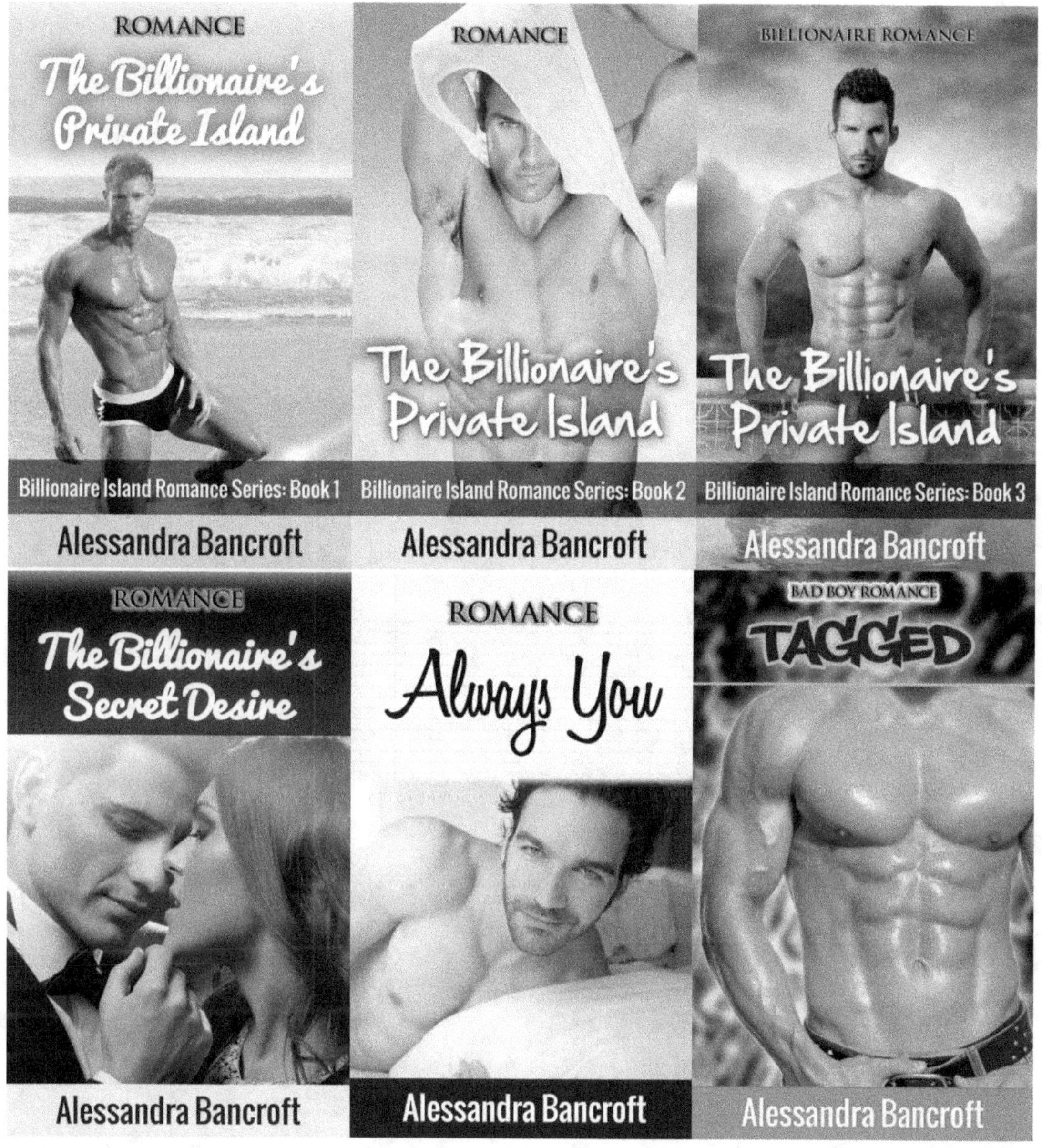

All of these are available in audio book as well.

If you enjoyed this book then please spare a few seconds to easily post a quick positive review. It would be greatly appreciated!

Thanks for reading.